Meera

the

Superhero

By Vanessa Porkins

Wherever there is a problem then they will get to see,

Whenever this takes place, whether at night or ten past three,

You might have seen one earlier as you enjoyed your fun-filled day,

Although you may not remember if they wipe your memories away,

Superheroes are special and they live in every town,

Making sure that they can help invert the deepest frown.

This story is about Superhero Meera who is one of the very best,

She wears a nice fitting outfit across her Superhero chest,

Her outfit is mostly red and pink and made of indestructible thread,

It's tear and stain resistant too and can even be worn in bed,

Her shoes have hidden lightning bolts which is why they are so fast,

Also wearing a deep long cape which she always puts on last.

Meera looked up and saw a woman carrying heavy shopping,

Rushing to her side and caught all that she was dropping,

With Superpowers enabled she lifted the bags and her up high,

Asking for directions Meera carried them to her house nearby,

Our girl delivered the shopping and the woman back to her abode,

After lots of thanks and chocolate she carried on down the road.

Meera came downstairs and looked at Mum who seemed very much upset,

"Granny is coming soon but the house is messy as I haven't had the chance to tidy yet",

With her Mum feeling tired and Granny on the drive she knew what was Mum's key need,

Zooming around the house and putting things in place using her incredible super speed,

Her Mum was shocked as Granny walked into a perfectly clean living room,

Not a hair out of place, a single speck of dust, or even a dirty spoon.

Meera looked out and saw something that was in the sky,

It was little Katie's kite that had escaped and had flown up high,

Zooming outside at speed and knowing what she must do,

Meera took off and flew up high chasing the kite whilst enjoying the view,

On capturing the escaped toy she returned back to the ground,

Handing back to Katie as she expressed a lovely 'Thank you' sound.

Mum took her girl to the bingo and told me she never wins,

Knowing this being a challenge despite the obvious sins!

Meera worked out exactly which numbers Mum needed on her card,

Sending telepathic messages to the caller who resisted her quite hard,

The numbers flowed exactly as she chose and Mum won the lot,

A very happy day out with winnings but not enough to buy a Yacht!

Meera wanted to spend the day playing games and stay in bed,

She needed to pretend she wasn't there but at a friend's place instead,

Using her Invisibility power she disappeared from everyone's view,

Although there were strange noises heard by Dad when he had to do a poo!

A nice sleepy fun day she had and enjoyed a lot of joy,

And when she reappeared again she was given a brand new toy!

A holiday to Australia is what Mummy wanted to do,

Although Daddy was scared of flying and always on the loo,

As they got ready for the trip, Meera zapped them with her mind,

Teleporting the family and leaving their home behind,

Sydney and the Kangaroos with a great holiday was had,

Even Daddy doesn't need the toilet quite so often or so bad!

The oven had broken just as mum was trying to cook a family dinner,

Everyone hungry with no food would make each a little thinner,

Meera took control and told everyone to sit down to relax or go and play,

She focused her eyes on the uncooked turkey and used a zapping heat-ray,

Her eyes cooked the meat and all the vegetables perfectly well,

And everyone loved the dinner and told our hero it was swell!

Looking at some photos of Meera's Great Great Grandfather,

She wanted to ask him questions face to face she would rather,

Using superhero time and space powers she travels back in time,

Greeting her long-lost relative for a chat right at their prime,

When she returned she seemed to understand the past much more,

Often talking in her sleep about her adventures before she would often snore.

As the days near the end, all Superheroes need to go to sleep,

Despite so many keen adventures and memories to keep,

Superheroes are definitely among us each and every day,

Meera is just one of those with powers in her special way,

To bed she goes with superpowers, her costume, and a lovely vest,

She is definitely one of the smallest but also one of the very best.

Enjoy being the Superhero you are!

Made in the USA
Monee, IL
14 March 2023

29852957R00017